HOUDINI

THE AMAZING CATERPILLAR

JANET PEDERSEN

CLARION BOOKS ✦ NEW YORK

"You will do amazing
and magical things, Houdini,"
whispered Houdini's mother when he was
just a tiny egg, nestled upon a bright green leaf.

Soon Houdini grew into a
caterpillar with bold stripes,
a big smile, and a hearty appetite!

And when he suddenly found himself in a new place with many curious faces peering at him, Houdini knew it was finally his moment to do amazing and magical things.

6

His audience loved him.

"And now, I will crawl across this high-wire stick . . . without falling!"

Ta-Da!

His audience made
drawings of him.

9

His audience brought him fresh leaves so he could do his vanishing act all over again. "Oooh! Ahhh!" they cried. Houdini smiled his big smile and bowed in appreciation. How he loved being in the spotlight!

But gradually, Houdini noticed his audience was becoming interested in other acts. When a turtle arrived, the crowd patiently waited for it to emerge from its shell. *Some performance,* thought Houdini with a yawn.

Then a spider showed up. Houdini couldn't understand what the big deal was, but the audience was as curious as ever. Houdini decided it was time to spice up his performances, to make them even more amazing.

Instead of just stepping out of his skin, Houdini rolled out.

He added a daring backflip to his high-wire-stick routine.

He performed his vanishing-leaf act with astonishing speed.

Every now and then a small audience gathered, but there were no longer the crowds. For the first time, Houdini felt neither amazing nor magical.

One night, under the light of
a full moon, Houdini munched
and thought. And thought and
munched. What could he do to
win back his audience? Looking
around, he had to admit the
turtle's new act showed courage.

The classroom plant was
a sight to behold.

And even though Houdini could
spot the thread, the spider's latest
trick was quite successful.

STAGE
1

Egg

STAGE
2

rpillar

Then he noticed something else. On the wall
before him were colorful drawings. They were
bright and bold, and they made Houdini smile.

Suddenly, he knew just what his next act
would be. It would be his most daring act ever!

It would take much concentration and skill, but Houdini felt ready. His audience would not want to miss it! Houdini broke free of his skin one last time.

Then he climbed to the very center
of the high-wire stick, and hung,
suspended in the air.

All that night . . .

. . . and all the next day, Houdini held his pose.
His audience discovered him.
They crowded around him.
They made new drawings
of him.

For almost two weeks,
Houdini held his pose

without food . . .

without water . . .

without taking a break . . .
and his audience
watched in anticipation.

Then one morning, Houdini opened his eyes. Many curious faces were peering at him. Houdini smiled his big smile, happy to be in the spotlight again!

"Gather close! This is the moment I will break free!"

Houdini twisted.

He squirmed.

"Oooh! Ahhh!" he heard as his new wings lifted him higher and higher. Houdini bowed his head in appreciation. He too was amazed—at the magic inside him.

AUTHOR'S NOTE

When my son was in kindergarten, his class learned about life cycles by watching caterpillars in a glass terrarium turn into butterflies. When the dozen or so butterflies had emerged from their chrysalises, the class held a "Butterfly Celebration Day" and released them outside. There was much joy and applause as the butterflies fluttered from flower to flower and beyond. It was a magical moment I will never forget, and it inspired this book. I named Houdini after the famous magician Harry Houdini, who was known for his daring, amazing performances, one of which was an escape act called "The Metamorphosis."

Monarch butterflies go through *metamorphosis*, which means change of form, in four stages:

1. Egg Stage: The adult butterfly lays her egg on a milkweed plant, which the caterpillar will eat once it hatches from the egg. The egg is very tiny, about the size of this period.

2. Caterpillar (Larva) Stage: When the caterpillar hatches from the egg, it is so small it can barely be seen, but it grows very fast. It eats and eats the leaves of the milkweed plant, stopping only when it needs to shed its outer layer of skin. This is called "molting," which happens when the caterpillar's body has gotten too big for its skin. When the caterpillar is fully grown, it sheds its final skin to reveal a jade-green casing, called a pupa, or chrysalis.

3. Chrysalis (Pupa) Stage: Although the chrysalis looks lifeless, there's a lot going on inside, as the caterpillar is literally liquefied and then reassembled. The cells of the body are being rearranged to form a butterfly's body.

4. Butterfly (Adult) Stage: When the butterfly is about to emerge, the chrysalis becomes transparent, revealing colors and patterns inside. Finally, the chrysalis splits, and a limp, damp butterfly emerges. It gathers strength as blood is pumped throughout its body. After about two hours, it's ready to take its first flight.

Life Cycle of the Monarch Butterfly
- - - - - - - - - -
Egg Stage: 3–4 Days
Caterpillar Stage: 14 days
Chrysalis Stage: 10 days
Butterfly Stage: 14–42 days

For Graham

Clarion Books • a Houghton Mifflin Company imprint • 215 Park Avenue South, New York, NY 10003 Copyright © 2008 by Janet Pedersen • The illustrations were executed in ink, watercolor, and digital media. • The text was set in 20-point Triplex Light. • All rights reserved. • For information about permission to reproduce selections from this book, write to Permissions, Houghton Mifflin Company, 215 Park Avenue South, New York, NY 10003. • www.clarionbooks.com • Manufactured in China Library of Congress Cataloging-in-Publication Data • Pedersen, Janet. • Houdini the amazing caterpillar / by Janet Pedersen. • p. cm. • Summary: A caterpillar does amazing tricks, like making leaves disappear and shedding its skin, and finally it performs the most amazing trick of all. Includes facts about the life cycle of the monarch butterfly. • ISBN 978-0-618-89332-4 • [1. Caterpillars—Fiction. 2. Metamorphosis—Fiction.] I. Title. • PZ7.P34233Ho 2008 • [E]—dc22 • 2007038138 • WKT 10 9 8 7 6 5 4 3 2 1